The Clumsy Giant

by Lynne Benton

Illustrated by Fabiano Fiorin

W
FRANKLIN WATTS
LONDON • SYDNEY

First published in 2015 by
Franklin Watts
338 Euston Road
London
NW1 3BH

Franklin Watts Australia
Level 17/207 Kent Street
Sydney
NSW 2000

A CIP catalogue record for this book is available from the British Library.

ISBN 978 1 4451 3786 5 (hbk)
ISBN 978 1 4451 3789 6 (pbk)
ISBN 978 1 4451 3788 9 (library ebook)
ISBN 978 1 4451 3787 2 (ebook)

Series Editor: Jackie Hamley
Series Advisor: Catherine Glavina
Series Designer: Peter Scoulding

Printed in China

Franklin Watts is a division of
Hachette Children's Books,
an Hachette UK company.
www.hachette.co.uk

Giant Bigfoot was clumsy.

He trod on cars.

"Oops!"

He bumped into houses.

He broke down bridges.

"Oh dear!"

"We must stop him!" said the people.

Peter the handyman had an idea.

He worked all night.

Next morning Peter climbed up the hill.

Soon Giant Bigfoot came along.

"These are for you,"
said Peter.

The giant put the glasses on.

"Oh!" he said. "Now I can see everything! Thank you, little man."

“Hooray!” said the people.

"Well done, Peter!"

Puzzle Time!

a

b

c

d

e

f

Put these pictures in the right order and tell the story!

worried

delighted

thrilled

nervous

Which words describe the people at the start of the story? Which describe them at the end?

Turn over for answers!

Notes for adults

TADPOLES are structured to provide support for newly independent readers. The stories may also be used by adults for sharing with young children.

Starting to read alone can be daunting. **TADPOLES** help by providing visual support and repeating words and phrases. These books will both develop confidence and encourage reading and rereading for pleasure.

If you are reading this book with a child, here are a few suggestions:

1. Make reading fun! Choose a time to read when you and the child are relaxed and have time to share the story.
2. Talk about the story before you start reading. Look at the cover and the blurb. What might the story be about? Why might the child like it?
3. Encourage the child to employ a phonics first approach to tackling new words by sounding the words out.
4. Invite the child to retell the story, using the jumbled picture puzzle as a starting point. Extend vocabulary with the matching words to pictures puzzle.
5. Give praise! Remember that small mistakes need not always be corrected.

Answers

Here is the correct order:

1.c 2.a 3.e 4.b 5.d 6.f

Words to describe the people at the start: nervous, worried

Words to describe them at the end: delighted, thrilled